MW00917307

Yvette,
A friend forever.
Love you, missing you.
Hope you enjoy the book.
Carol

# BEYOND THE MILES

**Carol Ann Brown**

authorHOUSE

*AuthorHouse™*
*1663 Liberty Drive*
*Bloomington, IN 47403*
*www.authorhouse.com*
*Phone: 1 (800) 839-8640*

*© 2016 Carol Ann Brown. All rights reserved.*

*No part of this book may be reproduced, stored in
a retrieval system, or transmitted by any means
without the written permission of the author.*

*Published by AuthorHouse    04/25/2016*

*ISBN: 978-1-5049-8475-1 (sc)*
*ISBN: 978-1-5049-8474-4 (e)*

*Library of Congress Control Number: 2016904304*

*Print information available on the last page.*

*Any people depicted in stock imagery provided by Thinkstock are
models, and such images are being used for illustrative purposes only.
Certain stock imagery © Thinkstock.*

*This book is printed on acid-free paper.*

*Because of the dynamic nature of the Internet, any web
addresses or links contained in this book may have changed
since publication and may no longer be valid. The views
expressed in this work are solely those of the author and do
not necessarily reflect the views of the publisher, and the
publisher hereby disclaims any responsibility for them.*

# INTRODUCTION

If this was a perfect world, there would not be racism, but since it isn't, let's face it racism still exists. I thank God that racism seems to be less prevalent with each passing decade. The characters in this story are two young people that grew up in the same rural community, but because of segregation in the south in the 50's and 60's, had no interaction. They both relocated to the north and as fate would have it, became a part of the same social circle, and fell in love.

This story shows that love is so powerful, that it expands beyond all barriers and overcome all obstacles, including racism. It also shows just how damaging racism is and how we as a society have to find a way to overcome racism.

# DEDICATION

This book is dedicated to my mother Matilda Brown-Ballard, who is 104 years young and has taught me by example never to give up on my dreams. My mother received her G.E.D. at age 56. My mother retired from working as a teacher's aid at the age of 93. My mother and father was married for 61 years, before he died in 1987. My mother mourned the death of my father for about six months, realized she wasn't ready to join him and formed a little league football team.

This book is also dedicated to my daughter and son-in-law, Ashley and William Pryor III. Also, to my son and daughter-in-law Sharnezz and Karole Brown and their three sons Joshua, Adam and Josiah Brown. I hope by writing this book, it will inspire my children and grandchildren to reach their god given potential, and to never give up on their dreams.

And finally, this book is dedicated to all the interracial couples that have the courage to follow their hearts.

# BEYOND THE MILES

## By Carol Ann Brown

Lawd ham mercy it's hot. Mama stopped hanging out clothes just long enough to take a small towel from her apron pocket and wipe the sweat from her face and neck. It was getting late, and Geraldine eagerly helped her mother hang out clothes, hoping that there would still be enough daylight left so the sun would dry their clothes before dark.

I don't understand, Mama, why you have to go to Ms. Jenny's to clean her house, and then have to come home and clean your own. Unwilling to accept the explanation that her mama gave her, Geraldine listened to it for the hundredth time. That's just the way it is baby, and then looking off into the distance as if the answer was out there some place, she repeated it again, that's just the way it is. After hanging out the clothes, Geraldine pumped water and heated it on the stove so she and her two little brothers could take baths. Jack, Jr. and Paul were much younger than Geraldine, and she often wondered why her parents waited so long to have other children. Geraldine loved her two brothers and often gave them their baths and helped her mother with her brothers.

While doing her homework, Geraldine would often daydream of what it would be like to live like the white people that her mother worked for. Geraldine would go to the big house with her mother on Saturdays. Ms. Jenny and Mr. Bill Simmons lived in the big house with their two children, Tricia and Billy. Geraldine would go to the window, and watch Tricia and Billy play tennis with their friends. Tricia was sixteen, and so was Geraldine. Billy was eighteen and finishing his last year in high school. Tricia, Billy and all their friends had cars. Geraldine wished that she was white, and one evening when sitting down to dinner, she made the mistake of saying it to her parents. Geraldine's mother, Josie, was a tiny woman with a powerful voice. She looked sternly at Geraldine and said she was never to feel that way, that she should be proud of her race. Geraldine's father a big, strong but quiet man, got up immediately without saying a word, and left the room. Geraldine knew what she said was awful, although she did not understand why. Geraldine thought anybody in their right mind would want to be white. She honestly thought that everyone felt that way. Why not? They lived in the big beautiful homes, while all the colored people that Geraldine knew lived in shacks. They drove the fine cars and were able to go off to college. Be proud of my race, Geraldine thought. What was there to be proud of? Proud to scrub white people floors, while they ran around and played tennis.

The next day, Geraldine's father, Jack Barnes, sat down with her at the table where Geraldine was doing her homework. He carefully searched for the right words to say. Geraldine, he said, no colored person want to live like this, and I would be lying if I said that working in the fields, while Mr. Simmons tell us when to go to work, and how long to work, didn't bother me. It bothers me plenty, but you have nothing to be shame of. We ain't done nothing wrong. It ain't a sin to be poor, but it is a sin not to try to do better. I got no schooling he said, and your mama got very little. That is why we try so hard to make sure that you stay in school. So that one day you can be somebody. So that one day you can make a difference. Looking at Geraldine with sad eyes he said, education is the only way, Geraldine, the only way.

Geraldine was a very good student, and she had dreams of going off to college, but she never thought they could be anything more than dreams. It took money to go to college, and they had none. Geraldine's father seemed to think it was possible, so for the first time she had hope. Also, something inside Geraldine had changed. Before when she went to the big house on Saturdays, she would look out of the window at the Simmons' two children, and she admired them. Now all she felt was resentment. She never knew that it was wrong to wish that she was white. Geraldine was living her life through them, and now that even that was taken away from her, she only felt hate for them.

Geraldine was not only a good student academically, but she was also very good in sports. She played softball very well and was number one in track at her school. Black schools were not allowed to participate in track meets, and they only competed against each other at the school.

Most families didn't have money to see a doctor, so the doctors and nurses would come to the school to immunize the students. One day a doctor came while the students were running track. He stood and watched as they ran. He had never seen anyone run as fast as Geraldine and another student, Lillian Petty, who was in Geraldine's junior class. He stood there clocking them over and over again; it was unbelievable. A few weeks later, two white men came to the school. They were college coaches and wanted to see the girls run.

The school principal called the two students into his office, and when Geraldine heard the news she was so excited her heart was pounding. She knew this was an opportunity of a lifetime. That day, not only did Geraldine beat every local high school record, but also every local college record. Geraldine was finally given the opportunity to go to college.

Geraldine rushed home from school with the great news. Josie ran through the house clapping her hands. Thank you Jesus, she said over and over again. Jack fell to his knees sobbing. Their prayers had been answered. There weren't any colleges in Mississippi at that time that had track competitions, so Geraldine was given a scholarship to Brownsdale College in Virginia.

Geraldine's first day of school was quite an experience. Unlike Geraldine's high school, which was an all black school, Brownsdale College was more diverse in ethnicity. Seventy-five percent of the students were white, twenty percent were black, and there were a few Asians. Geraldine was very excited that she was going to a school with people like Tricia and Billy. She had stood at Ms. Jenny's and watched them from the window socializing with their friends, and now she was actually attending a school with people like them. For the first time Geraldine felt equal to whites, but was soon brought back to reality when three white girls intentionally bumped into her and Lillian in the hallway, knocking Geraldine's books out of her hands. One of the girls said "Watch where you're going nigger." Geraldine was disappointed; she wasn't treated that badly in Mississippi.

After just a few days, Geraldine found out just how much racial tension was in Brownsdale between white students and black students. The Asians made sure to stay neutral. The racism between black and white students was so thick you could cut it with a knife. The black students sat together in the cafeteria, as did the white students. The Asian students kept to themselves. This was nothing like Geraldine imagined it to be. There were even white teachers that would make racial remarks against the black students in their class, and all the white students would laugh. Geraldine was determined not to let that interfere with her grades, nor her running track. This was an opportunity of a lifetime, and nothing was going to stand in her way. Geraldine and Lillian stayed to themselves. They didn't associate with the black students very much either. Almost every day, either the blacks were picking a fight with the white students, or vice versa. Geraldine and Lillian made a pact. They would keep to themselves and stay focused. Their only goal was to get an education, and nothing was going to get in their way. They knew that track had gotten them their scholarship, and they were determined to focus on those two things: keeping their grades up and doing well in track.

Geraldine and Lillian were the number one runners in track, which did not go over well with the white runners. One day during track, one of the white runners tripped Geraldine. Mr. Hansen, their coach, was not going to stand for it. He made the white student apologize. That day for about fifteen minutes, he made a speech that was so profound and intense you could hear a pin drop. For the first time Geraldine and Lillian felt that they had someone at the school that truly cared about them.

There was still tension between the black and white students, but Geraldine and Lillian felt more relaxed, and their performance on the track field was outstanding. They won every track meet. Geraldine would always win first place, and Lillian would always come in second. They even started to gain the respect of their fellow team members. Mr. Hansen always made sure that they had train tickets and could go home for the holidays. Geraldine and Lillian were celebrities in their home town. Whenever they would go into the grocery stores or the clothing stores, the owners of the stores would treat them with such respect, and ask them about school. They were actually the first students in their school that went off to college. They would see the black people in the stores, and on the street whispering and pointing to them, and they felt so proud. Yes, they were celebrities in their home town. They had a responsibility to the other students in their home town, and they were not about to let them down.

After four years of college, it was time for Geraldine to graduate. She felt very sad, because she was leaving Lillian behind. Lillian had another year to go, but Geraldine and Lillian had made such an impact and gained such respect at the school, that Geraldine knew that Lillian would be alright. It was time for graduation, and Mr. Hansen surprised Geraldine by sending for her parents, Jack and Josie Barnes. What a proud day it was for them. Not only did Geraldine graduate with honors, she received a standing ovation when her name was called to receive her degree. What a proud day it was for her parents. Geraldine had to pinch herself to make sure she wasn't dreaming. That day Jack and Josie, along with Lillian, were her biggest fans. Jack and Josie cried, while Lillian stood and applauded so long, someone had to sit her down. It was such a wonderful day. The ceremony was held outside in an open field. The day was bright and sunny, the grass was green, and Geraldine could feel the presence of God all around her. Yes, it was a perfect day, and Geraldine reveled in the glory of it all.

Geraldine was elated that she had received her B.A. degree, but there was an overwhelming desire to continue her education. She received a scholarship to Westlake University in Chicago to pursue her M.A degree. Because of her G.P.A. she was one of the first African American women to receive a full scholarship. Geraldine was very proud of her accomplishments, and so were her parents.

It was time to start a new life, and already Geraldine had offers from companies all over the United States. Geraldine had graduated with a degree in political science and decided to take a job teaching at Vonderville University in Chicago. Geraldine loved her job; it was worth everything she had endured to get there. Geraldine became very good friends with one of the white teachers at the university. Her name was Caroline, and she and Geraldine became inseparable. They had lunch together, went to movies together, and occasionally went dancing together. It was wonderful being able to go places together, and not having people look at them, or talking about them because of their race difference. They were good friends, enjoyed each other's company, and nobody seemed to mind.

Caroline was a member of a prestigious social club and invited Geraldine to go with her one night to an event that was given there. Geraldine was so excited. What would she wear? How would she fix her hair? Caroline and Geraldine shopped all day looking for just the right dress for Geraldine. After all Geraldine had never bought an evening dress. Even when they had social functions while in college, she never bothered to go. Her parents could not afford it, and that was alright with Geraldine. She was just happy to be in school, and to actually work toward getting a degree. Geraldine knew that social events would come later, and now it was time.

The day was spent preparing for the evening ahead. After all, every socialite in Chicago would be there. Caroline's family was very wealthy, and Caroline picked up Geraldine in a limousine. When Caroline saw Geraldine, her mouth fell opened. She never realized how beautiful Geraldine was. Geraldine was stunning. She looked like a black princess, and felt like one too.

They walked into the room, and Geraldine had never seen a place so beautiful. The room was elegant with white carpet, and furnished in colors of burgundy and gold. Every eye stared at Geraldine as she and Caroline walked into the room. John Paxton, a friend of Caroline's and a superior court judge, walked over to Caroline, and proceeded to talk to her as he attentively stared at Geraldine. "Oh John, I would like you to meet a very good friend of mine, Geraldine Barnes, she teaches at the University," said Caroline. John, already showing much attention to Geraldine as he talked to Caroline, held out his hand, and as Geraldine held out her hand he gently took her hand in his. "How do you do," he said to Geraldine with a warm smile. John Paxton was a very handsome man with high cheek bones and dark brown hair. He was very charming, and Geraldine found out later, that he was also married. His wife, blonde and very beautiful, came over introduced herself, and took John by the hand and led him across the room. Caroline looked at Geraldine, and they both chuckled.

About an hour into the evening, Geraldine was having the time of her life. She was dancing and meeting the kind of people that she had only read about. When Geraldine looked up, she saw Billy Simmons standing in the foyer. He was older, and more attractive, but it was Billy Simmons. Billy walked over to Caroline and kissed her on the cheek. After chatting briefly, Caroline turned to Geraldine, and introduced Billy to Geraldine. "Billy, I would like for you to meet a friend of mine Geraldine Barnes." Geraldine could tell that he did not recognize her. Billy asked Caroline to dance, but he kept staring at Geraldine. Geraldine was certain that Billy had finally recognized her, but later that evening as they were talking, Geraldine realized Billy Simmons did not remember her. Why would he? He never noticed her when she and her mother went to work for them. Billy Simmons did not recognize her, and that was fine with Geraldine. She was miles away from the world that she knew in Mississippi, and did not want anything to remind her.

Two months later, she and Caroline were having lunch in a restaurant on Michigan avenue, when who walked in but Billy Simmons, and one of his friends. "Is it o.k. if we join you?" the gentleman with Billy asked. Geraldine recognized him from the social club that she had attended with Caroline. His name was George Davis. He was African American, and Geraldine could not help but think how different things are in Chicago. In Mississippi, Billy Simmons wouldn't be caught dead with a black friend. It was a different world here alright, a very different world. Caroline said they would be delighted, and they sat and started to talk. After talking for a moment, Billy turned to Geraldine and focused his conversation toward her. It was intriguing getting to know the real Billy Simmons, the one she had admired from a distance.

One afternoon, Geraldine had just walked in the door from work when the phone rang. It was Billy apologizing for not having the nerves to ask her for her phone number. Somehow he had convinced Caroline to give it to him. He invited Geraldine to dinner, and although her first inclination was to say no, she heard herself say yes. Why not? She enjoyed his company, and besides, it was fascinating and exciting dating Billy, and him not knowing who she was. She had planned to tell him, but she had become rather fond of Billy and was afraid that he would think she was deceitful, and now she didn't know how to tell him.

Billy invited Geraldine to social gatherings, and Geraldine could tell Billy was becoming very fond of her. The feelings were mutual. After taking Geraldine home one evening from dinner, he kissed her. Geraldine was so frightened, she ran into her apartment, and didn't say goodnight. Once inside her apartment, Geraldine sat sobbing. How could she not see this coming? Now what would she do? How could she tell Billy that she was Geraldine Barnes from Mississippi. The Geraldine Barnes who had helped her mother clean their house and wash their clothes. Somehow she would have to tell him, and Geraldine prayed for the right words to say. But there were no words. Geraldine had fallen in love with Billy, and was sure that once he found out, she would lose him for sure. She would just have to take her chances. She had to let him know who she was.

Geraldine invited Billy for dinner at her place. They ate dinner by candlelight, and after dinner in front of a roaring fire, Geraldine exposed who she was. Billy sat there speechless. Geraldine was sure that he would go into a rage and tell her how deceitful she was and storm out, but none of that happened. After what seemed like an eternity, Billy turned to her and said, "Who you are, and what you did before I met you is not important. I didn't know you then, but I know you now, and I love you. It'll have to work itself out somehow." They sat there holding each other, knowing that they had to face the cruel world that awaited them back home.

After dating for about a year and becoming inseparable, Billy asked Geraldine to marry him. They were so in love, they could not imagine a life without each other, but they were from such a different

14

background, they could hardly imagine a life together. Billy had a hard time convincing Geraldine that they could make it work, but after a few months she agreed to marry him. They agreed not to tell their parents until after they were married. After all, their parents would only try to stop them. Billy and Geraldine had a small wedding ceremony in the garden at Caroline's parents' home. How Geraldine and Billy wished that their parents could have been there to witness their wedding day, but they knew that they had done the right thing. Now that they were married, their parents would have to accept it.

The time had come, and it was now time to tell their parents, and Geraldine thought that it would be easier to tell her parents. After all, they were Christian people and had always taught her to love everybody, certainly they would understand. Geraldine and Billy had been married for six months now, and with Christmas quickly approaching, Geraldine and Billy knew that it had to be done. They had to tell them, and hope for the best. Geraldine was three months pregnant, and they could not bring a child into the world and not have their parents be a part of it. Geraldine and Billy thought they would do it on Thanksgiving Day. That was a perfect time. It was a holiday, and everyone was happy and thankful. Surely this would be a great time to tell them.

Geraldine called her parents first, and they talked about how her brothers were all grown up and Paul her younger brother was in high school, and doing very well. Her older brother Jack, Jr. was in college. Yes, what she and Lillian had done had certainly made a difference in the town that she grew up in. It seemed that every black student was trying to follow their example. Winning track scholarships was the way most students went to college. Their school was known for winning track meets. There was even talk of some of the college students from their school trying for the Olympics.

After talking to her parents for a while, Geraldine could not bring herself to tell them that she had married Billy Simmons. How could she tell her parents, who had always been such an intimate part of her life that she had gotten married and not invited them to her wedding? And now to tell them that she was pregnant with their first grandchild and that she was married to Billy Simmons. The shock would just be too much for them over the phone. Geraldine thought we will just have to tell them when we go home for Christmas. Christmas was definitely a good time to tell them. Everyone's heart is filled with love during

Christmas. Yes, Geraldine thought, Christmas is a perfect time to tell them.

Jack and Josie Barnes were at the train station waiting anxiously for Geraldine. After all it had been over two years since they had seen her, and they could hardly wait. Geraldine stepped off the train, and Jack and Josie ran to meet her. Josie recognized Billy right away and thought that they just happened to be on the same train. "Mama, you remember Billy Simmons, Mr. Bill and Jenny Simmons' son?"

"Why yes I do. How are you Billy?"

"I am very well, thank you ma'am," Billy replied. Thank you ma'am, Josie thought, well he looks like young Billy. Things sure must be different up north.

Things were awkward and very uncomfortable for Geraldine and Billy. They stood there, the four of them. After for what seemed like a long time, although, it couldn't have been more than five minutes, Josie turned to Billy, and said to wish his parents a blessed holiday. Billy smiled, nodded and looked at Geraldine hoping that she would give him a clue of what they should do next. Geraldine said good-bye to Billy as Jack and Josie both grabbed her arms on either side, and whisked her away, as they told her of their plans for the best Christmas ever. Geraldine tried to share in the excitement and glory of it all. As she was being hurried away she looked over her shoulders to see Billy standing there with this puzzled look on his face. Then he slowly turned and walked away. Geraldine did not have a clue of what would happen next, but she loved Billy and he loved her and she knew that some how this would all work it self out.

Billy's arrival home was a pleasant surprise. It was a Saturday afternoon when he arrived, and Ms. Jenny's bridge club was meeting out on the veranda. Ms. Jenny looked up and saw Billy; she sat there for a moment in disbelief. "Billy, why didn't you tell us you were coming home?" She turned to her bridge club members. "Ya'll all know my boy Billy. I know ya'll will understand if I break this here up a little early, now won't you?" They all said they understood, and made a fuss over Billy and left.

"Now Mama you didn't have to break up your meeting because of me."

"Don't be silly Billy," Ms. Jenny said, looking at Billy with such pride in her eyes. "My boy, a big time lawyer in Chicago."

"I'm gonna go and take a shower," Billy said, and kissed his mother on the cheek.

In the shower Billy couldn't help but worry about the situation with him and Geraldine. Why, he missed her already. His heart was pounding so hard. There was no easy way to do this. He would just have to tell them, and it would be much easier to tell his mother while they were alone. Billy hurried and finished his shower, and was dressed in a matter of minutes. "Mother, I have something very important that I need to talk to you about."

"Why of course Billy, what is it?"

They were just about to sit down and talk when Mr. Bill Simmons walked in. He walked over to Billy, and hugged him and sat him down, and started to talk. Ms. Jenny was trying to explain to him that Billy had something important that he wanted to talk to her about.

"That's o.k. mama, we'll talk about it later."

Mr. Bill and Billy went for a walk, while Mr. Bill told Billy of all the changes that had taken place since he left. "Why don't you move back Billy, there is so much potential here for a young lawyer. The town's only got one lawyer, old man Pennebaker, and his boy

Jim. He's senile, and his boy is crazy as hell." Billy chuckled as he tried to tell his father he shouldn't talk that way. "No, but seriously, Billy, it would be good to have you home, son. Maybe you could think about settling down here and perhaps get married. Charlie Jenkins's daughter is back here, yes, she is helping her Daddy run the newspaper. Maybe we could invite her and her folks over for dinner while you are here." Nah, nah Daddy, Billy was stammering as thoughts of Geraldine, the marriage, the baby all ran through his mind. He had to think of a way to tell his parents, and it wasn't going to be easy. Maybe he would just let Geraldine tell her parents, and have them make such a fuss to his parents that he wouldn't have to tell them. No, Billy thought, that is a coward's way out. I will just have to tell them. After all, I am a grown man and they will just have to accept it.

Meanwhile, Geraldine was going out of her mind with worry. What if Billy suddenly changed his mind? What if he told his parents, and they talked him into a divorce? All the what-ifs ran through Geraldine's mind when the phone rang. Geraldine heard her mother say, sure Billy hold on she is right here. Geraldine ran into the room, as her mother handed her the phone with a puzzled look on her face. Geraldine took the phone into the other room and closed the door.

"Have you told them Geraldine?" he asked.

"No Billy, I just haven't had a chance. What about you? Did you tell your folks yet?"

"No, I was going to, but you know how it is."

"Yes, Billy I know how hard it is," Geraldine said sadly.

"But I'm going to tell them tonight right after dinner," Billy said. "How are you doing honey? Are you alright?"

"Yes Billy, I'm fine. I have been praying all day that God would help us get through this."

"Me too, Geraldine, and He will, it's gonna take a little time for everyone to accept it, that's all. It'll be alright you'll see. I miss you so much Geraldine. I don't know how long I can stay away from you."

"It'll be alright Billy, just take my picture to bed with you tonight, and I'll take yours, and we'll hold each other that way. I love you Billy."

"Me too, Geraldine."

"Why does it have to be this way Billy? Why should it matter because of the color of one's skin?"

"I don't know Geraldine, but it does not matter to God, and we've got him on our side, and I just know that somehow, we will get through this."

Ms. Jenny made all Billy's favorite foods and was disappointed when he didn't eat very much. "What's the matter Billy? Are you alright? You hardly touched your food, and I made everything that you like."

"I'm alright Mama." Billy cleared his throat.

"Are you sure you're alright? You're not coming down with something are you Billy?"

"No, I'm alright Mama." Billy cleared his throat again, and had just about got the nerves to tell them, when Ms. Jenny said that Tricia called, and said that she would be home tomorrow. "Isn't it exciting Billy? The whole family under one roof again."

"Yes Mama," Billy said, "very exciting." Ms. Jenny knew something was wrong, but she thought she'd better not pry. She would let his father talk to him tomorrow. Billy said that he was tired, and that he was turning in early. He said goodnight to his parents, and went to bed. He held Geraldine's picture close to him, and thought how foolish it was that the two of them had to be apart. They had taken their vows before God, and it was the happiest day of his life. Billy couldn't understand why he was feeling as if he had done something wrong. How could something so beautiful between two people turn into such an awkward situation?

The next day Geraldine woke up and ran to the bathroom. Josie could hear her throwing up. "Are you alright Geraldine?" Josie was standing outside the bathroom pleading with Geraldine to let her in. The phone rang, and it was Billy. This time Jack Barnes answered the phone. Geraldine, he said, Billy Simmons is on the phone and wants to speak to you. Geraldine came out of the bathroom looking awful.

"Geraldine are you alright? You want us to take you in to see Dr. Peters?"

"No Mama, I told you I'm alright." Geraldine took the phone from her father and went into her bedroom. Josie and Jack looked at each other, bewildered. Josie went into the kitchen and started breakfast. Geraldine came into the kitchen wearing her bathrobe. Josie knew something was very wrong. This was not like Geraldine at all. Geraldine had always gotten out of bed and right into the shower, and by the time Josie got breakfast on the table, she was dressed and ready to go. Josie also knew that if she pressured Geraldine, she would get absolutely nothing out of her. So she thought she would wait until Jack was off to work, and she would talk to her then.

Paul, her youngest brother, was still living at home and about to graduate from high school. Geraldine was happy when Paul came down to breakfast, because Geraldine didn't want her parents asking anymore questions. "So Mama tells me you are about to become a Morehouse man."

"Well, you know, what can I say, some of us just got it that way," Paul said as he pulled on his make belief beard.

"Yes, we'll see how you got it after the first semester," Geraldine said with a chuckle. "So when are Jack, Jr., Tina and JJ getting here Mama?" Geraldine was so happy to get Jack and Josie focus off of her. Jack, Jr. lived in Atlanta with his wife and son. Jack, Jr. had graduated from Morehouse, and had a successful accounting business in Atlanta. "They should get here by dinner time," Josie said.

After eating a piece of toast and orange juice, Geraldine felt better and went to get dressed. "Something is wrong Jack," Josie said. "I don't know what it is, but it has something to do with Billy Simmons. And why is he calling her?"

"Well, they traveled down on the train together," Jack said, "maybe he just wanted to say hello." Josie knew that something was going on between the two of them. She had a strong feeling that they didn't just happen to be on the same train. Josie knew when Jack and Paul went off to work she would have the whole day to get to the bottom of things. Jack worked at the lumber mill, and Paul helped out on Saturday. Geraldine tried hard to avoid being alone with Josie, but it seemed that everywhere Geraldine went, Josie was there. Geraldine knew she had to tell her family, but the longer she put it off, the more difficult it became. It was getting late, and Josie knew that soon Jack and Paul would be getting in from the lumber mill, and she wanted to find out what was going on before Jack, Jr. and his family arrived. "Geraldine," Josie said, "I was just wondering, I mean why?"

Geraldine ran to the window. "Why mama, it's Jack, Jr." Josie ran to the door, and opened it.

"You're early," she said, "we weren't expecting you til later." I mean I wanted to have dinner ready when you got here. Why, just look at you." Josie held JJ at arms length, and stepped back as to get a better look at him. "My! My!" she said, "you the spitting image of your daddy when he was your age. Come on in the house, dinner ain't ready yet, but I can get you something cold to drink."

"That's alright," Jack, Jr. said, "we aren't that hungry anyway. JJ had me stop every time he saw a fast food restaurant, and you know Tina when it comes to burgers and fries, she's as bad as JJ."

Jack, Jr., Tina and JJ went upstairs to take a shower and get unpacked. Things down here sure have changed mama, Geraldine said. Black people are building homes, and owning their own grocery stores. I mean, the black people homes are so beautiful, it's hard to tell the black people homes from the whites.

"Yes, we've come a long way," Josie said, "but we still got a ways to go."

"Yes, but things are a lot different then it was before I left," Geraldine said.

"Geraldine, what business you got with Billy Simmons calling here for you so much?" Josie blurted out. Geraldine did not anticipate the conversation taking a turn the way it did and was not prepared to answer Josie question. Geraldine stared at Josie with this bewildered look on her face. "Well, ain't you gonna answer me?" Josie said. Geraldine searched for the right words to say. Josie sat there eagerly waiting for an answer. Geraldine started to sob, and Josie could hardly understand a word she said, but she was sure she heard Geraldine mumble something about her and Billy being married. Thinking that she must have misunderstood what Geraldine had said, Josie came over to Geraldine, took her hand and asked slowly, "What did you say?"

"I said, Billy and I are married."

"Married?" Josie asked, and then she stammered, "How? Where? I mean, when?" Geraldine started to explain, and everything just started pouring out. Lawd ham mercy, Lawd ham mercy child, what you done went and done.

"Mama I wanted to tell you," Geraldine said. "I was just waiting for the right time!"

"The right time," Josie said angrily. "Well child, do Mr. Bill and Ms. Jenny Simmons know bout this?"

"I don't know, I mean I think so, Billy is going to tell them today."

Jack, Jr. and Tina heard the screaming and the sobbing and rushed into the kitchen. What's the matter Mama, he asked. What's going on? Josie sat there with this shocked look on her face, just staring at Geraldine in disbelief. What's wrong? Jack, Jr. asked again.

"Your sister just told me that she and Billy Simmons done got married."

"What are you talking about?" Jack, Jr. said to his mother, while turning toward Geraldine, and waiting for her to correct her mother. His mother must have misunderstood what Geraldine had said. After all, they hardly knew the Simmons, except that his mother worked for them while they were growing up. Surely his mother must have misunderstood Geraldine. At that moment, Jack and Paul walked in to see Geraldine sobbing, Josie sitting there in shock, and Jack, Jr. standing there with this puzzled look on his face. Tina stood quietly by the kitchen counter holding JJ close to her.

What in God's name is wrong, Jack asked? Geraldine looked up at her father hoping that he would at least listen to her, and started to explain. She told him the whole story how she had seen Billy Simmons at a social club, and how he didn't recognize her at first, and how she kept running into him. "It was fate daddy, can't you see, it was fate," she repeated herself. Jack Barnes was very attentive as Geraldine went on with her story, telling him how they fell in love and how they had wanted to invite them to their wedding, but thought it was best that they waited. Jack showed very little emotion as Geraldine went on to tell them that she was pregnant, and how happy she and Billy were. Josie blurted out, Happy! Happy! If you are so happy then tell me child where is your husband. Josie started to confirm Geraldine's worst fear by telling her that Billy's parents were not going to stand for him being married to a colored girl, and that they would convince him to divorce her, and that she would be stuck with having a mixed baby. She was about to go on, when Jack stopped her. Now Josie, you don't know if all that is true that you saying. Things are changing, and Mr. Bill and Ms. Jenny would have to consider that Geraldine is pregnant with their grandchild. You talking foolish Jack, you know it ain't no way that the Simmons goin' to 'cept no colored wife for Billy and no colored grandbaby. Geraldine ran into her bedroom and closed the door. What if her mother was right, what if she never saw Billy again. Geraldine was going on and on thinking of all the what-ifs when she heard her father say, come on in Billy. Geraldine ran into Billy's arms sobbing, and Billy held her close.

"Come on in Billy, and sit down," Jack Barnes said. Geraldine and Billy sat there passionately holding and kissing each other. The room was very quiet as the family heard Billy and Geraldine tell each other how much they loved each other and how they missed each other. It was impossible for anyone to sit and watch them together and not know that what they had was real. After a moment, Billy started to tell them the reaction of his parents after he told them the news.

His father went into a rage, while his mother sat there in shock. After a moment, Mr. Bill Simmons took a deep breath, and said it's alright, this can be fixed. You'll just have to get a divorce, and you can put the baby up for adoption.

"I hear that people up north do it all the time. Yes, everything is going to be alright it is not the end of the world. Nobody will ever have to know about this." And as if everything was settled, his father turned to Billy and said, don't worry I'll fix everything. Billy jumped up from the couch. What do you mean you will fix everything? I don't want you to fix nothing. Did you hear what I said? Geraldine and I are married, and we are in love, and we are having a baby, and you all will just have to accept it. "Accept it!," Mr. Bill said, "boy have you lost your mind? No well respected white man marries no nigger gal." Billy ran for the door his mother pleading for Billy to come back. His father said, "Let him go," and then screaming at Billy, he said, "and don't come back here until you have come to your senses. Until you get rid of this nigger wife and baby of yours, you are no longer a part of this family." Ms. Jenny, holding her hands over her ears and sobbing hysterically, begged Mr. Simmons not to talk to Billy like that. While Billy sat telling the story of what happened things were so quiet you could hear a pin drop. Jack Barnes stood up and walked over to Billy and Geraldine sitting on the couch, and said, we your family now, and I think everybody ought to just get some sleep, and we'll have a better outlook on things tomorrow.

The next day Jack and Josie and the family sat down with Billy and Geraldine, and said that after Christmas (which was the next day) they thought it would be a good idea if they went back to Chicago. They could come back and visit after the baby was born, and things had calmed down some. Give everybody a chance to think things through.

It was a year later and the baby was born, a little girl, and they named her Caitlin. Geraldine and Billy called to say that they were coming home for a visit. Josie and Jack were so excited. They could hardly wait to see their granddaughter for the first time. "I'll have to call Jack, Jr., and yes, I'll have to call and see if Paul can come home for the weekend." Slow down woman, Jack said with a smile. He tried to remain calm, but Josie could tell he was just as excited as she was. Paul called to say that he couldn't make it; he had to study for finals. Jack, Jr., Tina and JJ were excited to see the baby, and oh yes, Geraldine and Billy too.

Geraldine and Billy arrived on the afternoon train with their beautiful baby girl. People turned around and looked as they walked to Jack, Jr.'s car. They heard one couple say, ain't that Bill and Jenny's son, Billy? It's just a shame! What is this world coming to? Poor Bill and Jenny, to have their son married to a nigger.

Once inside Jack and Josie's home, they felt safe. It wasn't long before Billy and Geraldine realized that it wasn't just the whites talking, but blacks were talking too. One of their nosy neighbors, Ms. Sarah Givens, came over pretending that she wanted to borrow sugar. Josie met her at the door. "What can I do for you Sarah?" Josie asked.

"Just needed to borrow a lil sugar," Ms. Sarah said, while trying to peek over Josie's shoulder to look inside. Wait right here, I'll get some sugar for you, Josie said. Josie shut the screen door with Ms. Sarah outside as she went into the kitchen to get the sugar. Jack, Jack, Jr and Geraldine was laughing so hard they were in tears, while Ms. Sarah stood there hands cupped on either side of her face, with her face pressed tight against the screen trying to peep inside.

"I hear your daughter Geraldine is here. Sho would like to see her, why I ain't seen her since she was just a lil bitty sumthin."

"Well, maybe you can see her later," Josie said while pushing the cup of sugar out the door, and closing the door all at the same time. Now Josie, you know that wasn't a nice thing to do, Jack said, still laughing. Nobody thinking bout Sarah Givens, Josie said. She know she didn't want to borrow no sugar, Just trying to be nosy is all. Meanwhile, Billy missed the whole thing. Unsuccessful at his attempt to reach his parents, Billy came out of the dining room, and wondered what all the laughing was about, and as Geraldine started to tell him the story, she suddenly stopped, because she saw the sad look in Billy's eyes.

"Don't worry Billy," she said, "they'll come around," she repeated herself, "you'll see they'll come around."

Oh! how Billy wished that his mother could see his beautiful baby girl.

Three days had passed since Geraldine and Billy came home, and already Geraldine was dreading having to say goodbye to her family. Geraldine and Billy would leave for Chicago in three days. Although she and Billy had encountered stares and rude comments from ignorant prejudice people, it was still home, and Geraldine enjoyed the smell of magnolia blossoms, the smell of the rich Mississippi dirt after a spring shower, the sound of robins chirping as they sat perched in the china berry trees, and the sound of laughter as neighbors sat on their porch at dusk, and watching the children play hide go seek.

As Geraldine sat out on the screened in porch, she couldn't help but reminisce back on her childhood. Now that she looked back on it, growing up in Mississippi was not so bad. Whatever was lacking in her life in the way of material wealth was more than compensated for in love. Geraldine wished that she lived closer to her parents so that they could watch Caitlin grow up. We'll just have to come home every year, Geraldine thought.

The next day Geraldine and Billy was sitting outside enjoying the afternoon breeze while watching Caitlin run around enjoying the open space, when Ms. Jenny drove up. Billy and Geraldine could not believe their eyes. She explained that she could not stay long because Mr. Simmons would die if he knew that she had come for a visit. Could you sit and visit for just a few minutes, Geraldine asked. Well, maybe I'll sit for just a few minutes, said Ms. Jenny. She had not taken her eyes off Caitlin from the time she walked into the yard.

"Go ahead mama you can hold her," Billy said, "She is your granddaughter." Ms. Jenny walked over to Caitlin, and took her in her arms, and for a moment it seemed that the world that surrounded them was absolutely color blind. All that was felt was love. There were no white or black, just granddaughter and grandmother enjoying each other, while son and daughter-in-law looked on.

Five years had past, and Caitlin was now six years old when Billy and Geraldine received a letter from Ms. Jenny stating that Billy's father had been diagnosed with leukemia, and if Billy could come home to be tested right away. The doctor's had given him less than a year to live if they didn't find a matching donor. Although, Billy hadn't spoken to his father in five years, he had stayed in touch with his mother. Whenever they went home to visit Geraldine's parents, Ms. Jenny would come over to visit with her son and his family. Mr. Bill never knew that his wife stayed in touch with their son, and Ms. Jenny knew she could never let him know. Ms. Jenny adored Caitlin, and had now become fond of Geraldine, but Mr. Bill never accepted his daughter-in-law and grandchild and wanted nothing to do with Billy as long as he stayed with them. Billy was committed to his wife and child, and although he missed his father, he came to terms that he would never have a relationship with him again. When Ms. Jenny called to tell Billy about his father, and to ask him if he could be tested for a bone marrow donor, Billy was furious.

"How could you ask me to be tested?" exclaimed Billy. "My father hasn't spoken to me in five years, and has never laid eyes on his granddaughter." Billy apologized to his mother for getting so angry, but said he could not be tested. Ms. Jenny slowly hang up the phone and thought how close Billy and his father had once been. Although she knew Billy had every right to feel the way that he felt about his father, this was still his father, and she knew that Billy still loved him and would never forgive himself if his father died, and he hadn't tried to help.

The next day Ms. Jenny called Geraldine to try to persuade her to talk to Billy. Geraldine tried to understand what she was saying, but it was difficult to understand through all of the sobbing. Finally, Geraldine got her to calm down, and Ms. Jenny realized Geraldine didn't have a clue of what she was talking about. She could not believe that Billy hadn't bothered to discuss this with his wife. Ms. Jenny asked Geraldine to promise that she would talk to Billy and try to convince him that being tested was the right thing to do.

Geraldine agreed with her that he should, and promised her that she would talk to Billy about it that night. Geraldine wasn't sure how to approach Billy. It would have been much easier if he had approached her about it, but he didn't. She knew that she had to find a way. That night while eating dinner, Geraldine mentioned to Billy that his mother had called, and wanted her to speak to him about being tested. She thought that he should.

"How could you even suggest that I do this?" Billy exclaimed. "He never accepted you, and he has never even seen his granddaughter."

After pleading with Billy for hours, Geraldine finally convinced him. You don't have to necessarily do it for him Billy, she said, but do it so that you can live with yourself. Billy agreed that he would, and called to tell his mother that he would be there the following week. His mother had hope again. Tricia had been tested and was not found to be a match. The same happened with Mr. Bill's two brothers and sister. They had gone to the local churches and asked the congregations if they would be tested. They even did television commercials trying to find donors. The townspeople were very responsive, but with all their efforts, they had failed to find a suitable donor for Mr. Bill. Time was running out, and Billy seemed to be their last hope.

The following week Billy arrived at the train station, and Tricia eagerly waited to meet him. Billy and Tricia didn't see each other often, because Tricia lived in Washington, and was very busy in politics. Billy was happy that Tricia was home. Somehow, he thought it would make things easier, but as soon as Billy told Tricia that he was willing to be tested but did not want to see his father, Tricia became hysterical. To make matters worse, Tricia made the mistake of saying to Billy that he was stubborn just like his father. Billy asked to be dropped off at the hotel where he was staying, and said that he would be leaving right after he was tested the next day. Tricia knew that Billy was hurting badly, and she also knew that Billy wanted to see his father. Why else would he have come all the way from Chicago? After all, he could have been tested in Chicago, and the results sent home. She also knew that Billy's father wanted to see him, but with the two of them being so stubborn it would never happen unless Tricia figured out a way. Tricia called the hospital to find out the time of Billy's appointment, and she and Ms. Jenny decided to tell his father that the hospital needed him to come in for an appointment at the same time. They just had to find a way to get the two of them together.

After being tested, Billy walked out of the room, and as he was walking down the hall, Mr. Bill stood up as he called out, "Billy is that you?" Billy turned around, and seeing his father standing there looking much older and very thin, tears streamed down his cheeks. Mr. Bill walked toward Billy in disbelief, and when he reached Billy, the two embraced and they stood there for minutes holding each other and sobbing. Mr. Bill convinced Billy to come to the house for dinner. It was wonderful having the four of them together again. Ms. Jenny brought out photographs of Billy and Tricia as children. After looking at old photographs and reminiscing, Billy reached in his coat pocket opened his wallet and took out a picture of him, Geraldine and Caitlin, and handed it to his father. Mr. Bill threw the picture on the floor, and left the room. Billy said good-bye to his mother and sister, and said they knew how to reach him and to stay in touch. Vowing that he never wanted to see his father again, he stormed out of the house.

After a few weeks, the phone rang. Geraldine handed the phone to Billy, and Ms. Jenny announced that his test results were back, and that he was not a match. Billy had mixed emotions. He had hoped that he would be a match, so he was somewhat disappointed, but on the other hand, he thought that was God's way of punishing his father for not accepting his family. He hoped that his father would realize that and change his ways.

A few months passed, and Ms. Jenny had call to say that Mr. Bill was back in the hospital, and to ask if they would consider letting Caitlin be tested. Both Billy and Geraldine said absolutely not. After hanging up the phone, they sat there in shock. How could she even fix her mouth to ask them to let Caitlin be tested? He had never even seen Caitlin. Why, if he saw her walking on the streets, he would not know her. They agreed that no way would they even consider letting her be tested, and the discussion was closed.

Geraldine found herself waking up in the middle of the night feeling badly about their decision. She could not understand it. She knew they had every right to feel the way that they felt. He was wrong, and they were right, so why did she feel so guilty? Geraldine tried everything that she could to dismiss the thoughts that kept haunting her. After a few weeks she hardly slept at all. After praying about it, Geraldine knew that she had to convince Billy to let Caitlin be tested.

Geraldine approached Billy and asked him to reconsider their decision. The worse scene that she had imagined was small in comparison to the scenario that actually took place. Billy was so angry that it frightened Geraldine. He had turned cold and bitter. What happened to the wonderful, sensitive, and compassionate man that she had married? Geraldine knew that in order to get back the man that she had married, she had to somehow convince Billy to let Caitlin be tested. Geraldine continued to pray about the situation, and one night she woke up to find Billy standing and staring out the window into the dark night. Billy was hardly sleeping, as well. Geraldine noticed that he wasn't eating. She knew that God was dealing with Billy, and she just kept praying and waiting.

One morning while Geraldine was preparing breakfast, Billy walked over to her, took her by the hand, and sat her down. He looked into her eyes and thanked her for sharing her life with him. He knew that Geraldine's faith and prayers had helped him make the decision that would save his soul from torment forever, and he agreed to let Caitlin be tested as a donor for his father. They stood there holding each other and thanking God for giving them the strength to do the right thing.

After calling his mother and giving her the news, they made plans for Caitlin to be tested. Mr. Bill was very ill now, and although Billy and his father had a bad relationship, Billy knew that his mother needed him and that the family should be together now. They decided to have Caitlin tested in Mississippi and wait for the results with his family.

It was early winter when they arrived in Mississippi, and as they walked into the entrance of Jack and Josie Barnes's home, Geraldine smelled the aroma of baked bread mixed with pine. Her father always used pine to start the fire in the oversized fireplace. Geraldine loved the winters in Mississippi. She walked out into the back yard, and memories of her childhood flooded her mind as she looked at the tall chinaberry trees that now were totally bare. Geraldine used to sit for hours as a child looking past the trees into the sky, imagining the kind of life that existed far beyond the open fields. Geraldine was engrossed in childhood memories and was brought back to reality when Billy yelled out the backdoor to tell her that it was time to take Caitlin to the hospital.

Caitlin was only six, and although she did not understand exactly what was happening, she knew that what she was about to do was very important. Geraldine and Billy explained to her that her grandfather who she had never met was sick and that perhaps she could help him. Caitlin was tested, and after only four days, Geraldine and Billy received a call from the hospital asking them to come in to meet with his father's doctor. The doctor came out to meet them, and by the excited look on his face, Billy knew that Caitlin was a matching donor. The doctor explained that Caitlin should be admitted into the hospital as soon as possible. Geraldine just stood there, although she could hear them talking, her mind was so bombarded with thoughts of Caitlin, and how young she was and what if something went wrong, she could not understand a word they were saying. It's as if she was inside a box, and she could hear everything around her but she could not participate. She just stood there in a state of shock. When Billy said is that all right with you Geraldine, she stood there unable to speak. Geraldine stammered, "Sure Billy, whatever you say," she managed to say eventually, before they slowly walked down the corridor.

When Billy arrived at the home of his in-laws, he called to give his mother the good news. She sobbed uncontrollably as Billy told her how Caitlin was a perfect match and the doctor had scheduled her for surgery the next day.

Mr. Bill's surgery was a success, and he was now home, recovering quite well. One morning Ms. Jenny went into the room to check on him, and he asked her to sit down. He hesitated for a moment, and then said that he wanted her to call Billy. Ms. Jenny sat there in disbelief, but after a few minutes reached for the telephone to call Billy.

Geraldine had just put dinner on the table, and the three of them were about to have dinner when the telephone rang. Geraldine answered the phone, and to her amazement it was Mr. Bill on the line. He introduced himself, and asked how Caitlin was. Billy stood up from the table when he heard Geraldine say, very well, thank you, Mr. Bill.

Geraldine gave the phone to Billy. Mr. Bill told Billy that as soon as he was able, that he would love to have the three of them come for a visit.

"Why sure dad," Billy said stammering. "Are you sure that you want the entire family to come?"

Mr. Bill said that he was sure, and that he could not wait to meet Geraldine and Caitlin. When he hang up the phone, Ms. Jenny held out her hands, arms stretched wide, held her husband, and told him how happy he had made her.

Meanwhile, Geraldine and Billy stood in absolute shock. When it dawned on them what had happened, they started to dance around the room. Caitlin saw her mom and dad dancing and laughing through tears, and she joined them. It was the happiest day of their lives. Geraldine and Billy were so happy that they had obeyed God. Because of their forgiving hearts and willingness to allow Caitlin to be tested, they could all be a family.

*The End*

CPSIA information can be obtained
at www.ICGtesting.com
Printed in the USA
FSOW01n1512190516
20626FS

9 781504 984751